Book Title

Author   Nationality

Genre   Year   Pages

Memorable Quote	Page Number

Characters

Plot Summary

Notes

Rating ☆ ☆ ☆ ☆ ☆

Book Title

Author

Nationality

Genre

Year

Pages

Memorable Quote	Page Number

Characters

Plot Summary

Notes

Rating ☆ ☆ ☆ ☆ ☆

Book Title

Author

Nationality

Genre

Year

Pages

Memorable Quote	Page Number

Characters

Plot Summary

Notes

Rating ☆ ☆ ☆ ☆ ☆

Book Title

Author ______________________   Nationality ______________

Genre ______________________   Year ______________   Pages ______

Memorable Quote	Page Number

Characters

Plot Summary

Notes

Rating ☆ ☆ ☆ ☆ ☆

Book Title

Author

Nationality

Genre

Year

Pages

Memorable Quote	Page Number

Characters

Plot Summary

Notes

Rating ☆ ☆ ☆ ☆ ☆

Book Title

Author

Nationality

Genre

Year

Pages

Memorable Quote	Page Number

Characters

Plot Summary

Notes

Rating ☆ ☆ ☆ ☆ ☆

Book Title

Author

Nationality

Genre

Year

Pages

Memorable Quote	Page Number

Characters

Plot Summary

Notes

Rating ☆ ☆ ☆ ☆ ☆

Book Title

Author   Nationality

Genre   Year   Pages

Memorable Quote	Page Number

Characters

Plot Summary

Notes

Rating ☆ ☆ ☆ ☆ ☆

Book Title

Author

Nationality

Genre

Year

Pages

Memorable Quote	Page Number

Characters

Plot Summary

Notes

Rating ☆ ☆ ☆ ☆ ☆

Book Title

Author

Nationality

Genre

Year

Pages

Memorable Quote	Page Number

Characters

Plot Summary

Notes

Rating ☆ ☆ ☆ ☆ ☆

Book Title

Author

Nationality

Genre

Year

Pages

Memorable Quote	Page Number

Characters

Plot Summary

Notes

Rating ☆ ☆ ☆ ☆ ☆

Book Title

Author

Nationality

Genre

Year

Pages

Memorable Quote	Page Number

Characters

Plot Summary

Notes

Rating ☆ ☆ ☆ ☆ ☆

Book Title

Author

Nationality

Genre

Year

Pages

Memorable Quote	Page Number

Characters

Plot Summary

Notes

Rating ☆ ☆ ☆ ☆ ☆

Book Title

Author

Nationality

Genre

Year

Pages

Memorable Quote	Page Number

Characters

Plot Summary

Notes

Rating ☆ ☆ ☆ ☆ ☆

Book Title

Author

Nationality

Genre

Year

Pages

Memorable Quote	Page Number

Characters

Plot Summary

Notes

Rating ☆ ☆ ☆ ☆ ☆

Book Title

Author

Nationality

Genre

Year

Pages

Memorable Quote	Page Number

Characters

Plot Summary

Notes

Rating ☆ ☆ ☆ ☆ ☆

Book Title

Author

Nationality

Genre

Year

Pages

Memorable Quote	Page Number

Characters

Plot Summary

Notes

Rating ☆ ☆ ☆ ☆ ☆

Book Title

Author

Nationality

Genre

Year

Pages

Memorable Quote	Page Number

Characters

Plot Summary

Notes

Rating ☆ ☆ ☆ ☆ ☆

Book Title

Author

Nationality

Genre

Year

Pages

Memorable Quote	Page Number

Characters

Plot Summary

Notes

Rating ☆ ☆ ☆ ☆ ☆

Book Title

Author

Nationality

Genre

Year

Pages

Memorable Quote	Page Number

Characters

Plot Summary

Notes

Rating ☆ ☆ ☆ ☆ ☆

Book Title

Author

Nationality

Genre

Year

Pages

Memorable Quote	Page Number

Characters

Plot Summary

Notes

Rating ☆ ☆ ☆ ☆ ☆

Book Title

Author

Nationality

Genre

Year

Pages

Memorable Quote	Page Number

Characters

Plot Summary

Notes

Rating ☆ ☆ ☆ ☆ ☆

Book Title

Author   Nationality

Genre   Year   Pages

Memorable Quote	Page Number

Characters

Plot Summary

Notes

Rating ☆ ☆ ☆ ☆ ☆

Book Title

Author

Nationality

Genre

Year

Pages

Memorable Quote	Page Number

Characters

Plot Summary

Notes

Rating ☆ ☆ ☆ ☆ ☆

Book Title

Author

Nationality

Genre

Year

Pages

Memorable Quote	Page Number

Characters

Plot Summary

Notes

Rating ☆ ☆ ☆ ☆ ☆

Book Title

Author

Nationality

Genre

Year

Pages

Memorable Quote	Page Number

Characters

Plot Summary

Notes

Rating ☆ ☆ ☆ ☆ ☆

Book Title

Author   Nationality

Genre   Year   Pages

Memorable Quote	Page Number

Characters

Plot Summary

Notes

Rating   ☆ ☆ ☆ ☆ ☆

Book Title

Author

Nationality

Genre

Year

Pages

Memorable Quote	Page Number

Characters

Plot Summary

Notes

Rating ☆ ☆ ☆ ☆ ☆

Book Title

Author

Nationality

Genre

Year

Pages

Memorable Quote	Page Number

Characters

Plot Summary

Notes

Rating ☆ ☆ ☆ ☆ ☆

Book Title

Author

Nationality

Genre

Year

Pages

Memorable Quote	Page Number

Characters

Plot Summary

Notes

Rating ☆ ☆ ☆ ☆ ☆

Book Title

Author

Nationality

Genre

Year

Pages

Memorable Quote	Page Number

Characters

Plot Summary

Notes

Rating ☆ ☆ ☆ ☆ ☆

Book Title

Author

Nationality

Genre

Year

Pages

Memorable Quote	Page Number

Characters

Plot Summary

Notes

Rating ☆ ☆ ☆ ☆ ☆

Book Title

Author

Nationality

Genre

Year

Pages

Memorable Quote	Page Number

Characters

Plot Summary

Notes

Rating ☆ ☆ ☆ ☆ ☆

Book Title

Author

Nationality

Genre

Year

Pages

Memorable Quote	Page Number

Characters

Plot Summary

Notes

Rating ☆ ☆ ☆ ☆ ☆

Book Title

Author

Nationality

Genre

Year

Pages

Memorable Quote	Page Number

Characters

Plot Summary

Notes

Rating ☆ ☆ ☆ ☆ ☆

Book Title

Author

Nationality

Genre

Year

Pages

Memorable Quote	Page Number

Characters

Plot Summary

Notes

Rating ☆ ☆ ☆ ☆ ☆

Book Title

Author

Nationality

Genre

Year

Pages

Memorable Quote	Page Number

Characters

Plot Summary

Notes

Rating ☆ ☆ ☆ ☆ ☆

Book Title

Author

Nationality

Genre

Year

Pages

Memorable Quote	Page Number

Characters

Plot Summary

Notes

Rating ☆ ☆ ☆ ☆ ☆

Book Title

Author

Nationality

Genre

Year

Pages

Memorable Quote	Page Number

Characters

Plot Summary

Notes

Rating ☆ ☆ ☆ ☆ ☆

Book Title

Author   Nationality

Genre   Year   Pages

Memorable Quote	Page Number

Characters

Plot Summary

Notes

Rating ☆ ☆ ☆ ☆ ☆

Book Title

Author

Nationality

Genre

Year

Pages

Memorable Quote	Page Number

Characters

Plot Summary

Notes

Rating ☆ ☆ ☆ ☆ ☆

Book Title

Author

Nationality

Genre

Year

Pages

Memorable Quote	Page Number

Characters

Plot Summary

Notes

Rating ☆ ☆ ☆ ☆ ☆

Book Title

Author

Nationality

Genre

Year

Pages

Memorable Quote	Page Number

Characters

Plot Summary

Notes

Rating ☆ ☆ ☆ ☆ ☆

Book Title

Author   Nationality

Genre   Year   Pages

Memorable Quote	Page Number

Characters

Plot Summary

Notes

Rating ☆ ☆ ☆ ☆ ☆

Book Title

Author   Nationality

Genre   Year   Pages

Memorable Quote	Page Number

Characters

Plot Summary

Notes

Rating ☆ ☆ ☆ ☆ ☆

Book Title

Author

Nationality

Genre

Year

Pages

Memorable Quote	Page Number

Characters

Plot Summary

Notes

Rating ☆ ☆ ☆ ☆ ☆

Book Title

Author

Nationality

Genre

Year

Pages

Memorable Quote	Page Number

Characters

Plot Summary

Notes

Rating ☆ ☆ ☆ ☆ ☆

Book Title

Author ____________________ Nationality ____________________

Genre ____________________ Year ____________________ Pages ________

Memorable Quote	Page Number

Characters

Plot Summary

Notes

Rating ☆ ☆ ☆ ☆ ☆

Book Title

Author

Nationality

Genre

Year

Pages

Memorable Quote	Page Number

Characters

Plot Summary

Notes

Rating ☆ ☆ ☆ ☆ ☆

Book Title

Author

Nationality

Genre

Year

Pages

Memorable Quote	Page Number

Characters

Plot Summary

Notes

Rating ☆ ☆ ☆ ☆ ☆

Book Title

Author

Nationality

Genre

Year

Pages

Memorable Quote	Page Number

Characters

Plot Summary

Notes

Rating ☆ ☆ ☆ ☆ ☆

Book Title

Author

Nationality

Genre

Year

Pages

Memorable Quote	Page Number

Characters

Plot Summary

Notes

Rating ☆ ☆ ☆ ☆ ☆

Book Title

Author

Nationality

Genre

Year

Pages

Memorable Quote	Page Number

Characters

Plot Summary

Notes

Rating ☆ ☆ ☆ ☆ ☆

Book Title

Author

Nationality

Genre

Year

Pages

Memorable Quote	Page Number

Characters

Plot Summary

Notes

Rating ☆ ☆ ☆ ☆ ☆

Book Title

Author

Nationality

Genre

Year

Pages

Memorable Quote	Page Number

Characters

Plot Summary

Notes

Rating ☆ ☆ ☆ ☆ ☆

Book Title

Author

Nationality

Genre

Year

Pages

Memorable Quote	Page Number

Characters

Plot Summary

Notes

Rating ☆ ☆ ☆ ☆ ☆

Book Title

Author

Nationality

Genre

Year

Pages

Memorable Quote	Page Number

Characters

Plot Summary

Notes

Rating ☆ ☆ ☆ ☆ ☆

Book Title

Author   Nationality

Genre   Year   Pages

Memorable Quote	Page Number

Characters

Plot Summary

Notes

Rating ☆ ☆ ☆ ☆ ☆

Book Title

Author   Nationality

Genre   Year   Pages

Memorable Quote	Page Number

Characters

Plot Summary

Notes

Rating ☆ ☆ ☆ ☆ ☆

Book Title

Author   Nationality

Genre   Year   Pages

Memorable Quote	Page Number

Characters

Plot Summary

Notes

Rating ☆ ☆ ☆ ☆ ☆

Book Title

Author

Nationality

Genre

Year

Pages

Memorable Quote	Page Number

Characters

Plot Summary

Notes

Rating ☆ ☆ ☆ ☆ ☆

Book Title

Author

Nationality

Genre

Year

Pages

Memorable Quote	Page Number

Characters

Plot Summary

Notes

Rating ☆ ☆ ☆ ☆ ☆

Book Title

Author ___________________ Nationality ___________________

Genre ___________________ Year ___________________ Pages ___________

Memorable Quote	Page Number

Characters

Plot Summary

Notes

Rating ☆ ☆ ☆ ☆ ☆

Book Title

Author

Nationality

Genre

Year

Pages

Memorable Quote	Page Number

Characters

Plot Summary

Notes

Rating ☆ ☆ ☆ ☆ ☆

Book Title

Author

Nationality

Genre

Year

Pages

Memorable Quote	Page Number

Characters

Plot Summary

Notes

Rating 

Book Title

Author

Nationality

Genre

Year

Pages

Memorable Quote	Page Number

Characters

Plot Summary

Notes

Rating ☆ ☆ ☆ ☆ ☆

Book Title

Author

Nationality

Genre

Year

Pages

Memorable Quote	Page Number

Characters

Plot Summary

Notes

Rating ☆ ☆ ☆ ☆ ☆

Book Title

Author

Nationality

Genre

Year

Pages

Memorable Quote	Page Number

Characters

Plot Summary

Notes

Rating ☆ ☆ ☆ ☆ ☆

Book Title

Author

Nationality

Genre

Year

Pages

Memorable Quote	Page Number

Characters

Plot Summary

Notes

Rating ☆ ☆ ☆ ☆ ☆

Book Title

Author

Nationality

Genre

Year

Pages

Memorable Quote	Page Number

Characters

Plot Summary

Notes

Rating ☆ ☆ ☆ ☆ ☆

Book Title

Author

Nationality

Genre

Year

Pages

Memorable Quote	Page Number

Characters

Plot Summary

Notes

Rating ☆ ☆ ☆ ☆ ☆

Book Title

Author

Nationality

Genre

Year

Pages

Memorable Quote	Page Number

Characters

Plot Summary

Notes

Rating ☆ ☆ ☆ ☆ ☆

Book Title

Author

Nationality

Genre

Year

Pages

Memorable Quote	Page Number

Characters

Plot Summary

Notes

Rating ☆ ☆ ☆ ☆ ☆

Book Title

Author

Nationality

Genre

Year

Pages

Memorable Quote	Page Number

Characters

Plot Summary

Notes

Rating ☆ ☆ ☆ ☆ ☆

Book Title

Author   Nationality

Genre   Year   Pages

Memorable Quote	Page Number

Characters

Plot Summary

Notes

Rating ☆ ☆ ☆ ☆ ☆

Book Title

Author   Nationality

Genre   Year   Pages

Memorable Quote	Page Number

Characters

Plot Summary

Notes

Rating ☆ ☆ ☆ ☆ ☆

Book Title

Author

Nationality

Genre

Year

Pages

Memorable Quote	Page Number

Characters

Plot Summary

Notes

Rating ☆ ☆ ☆ ☆ ☆

Book Title

Author

Nationality

Genre

Year

Pages

Memorable Quote	Page Number

Characters

Plot Summary

Notes

Rating ☆ ☆ ☆ ☆ ☆

Book Title

Author

Nationality

Genre

Year

Pages

Memorable Quote	Page Number

Characters

Plot Summary

Notes

Rating ☆ ☆ ☆ ☆ ☆

Book Title

Author

Nationality

Genre

Year

Pages

Memorable Quote	Page Number

Characters

Plot Summary

Notes

Rating ☆ ☆ ☆ ☆ ☆

Book Title

Author

Nationality

Genre

Year

Pages

Memorable Quote	Page Number

Characters

Plot Summary

Notes

Rating ☆ ☆ ☆ ☆ ☆

Book Title

Author

Nationality

Genre

Year

Pages

Memorable Quote	Page Number

Characters

Plot Summary

Notes

Rating ☆ ☆ ☆ ☆ ☆

Book Title

Author

Nationality

Genre

Year

Pages

Memorable Quote	Page Number

Characters

Plot Summary

Notes

Rating ☆ ☆ ☆ ☆ ☆

Book Title

Author   Nationality

Genre   Year   Pages

Memorable Quote	Page Number

Characters

Plot Summary

Notes

Rating ☆ ☆ ☆ ☆ ☆

Book Title

Author   Nationality

Genre   Year   Pages

Memorable Quote	Page Number

Characters

Plot Summary

Notes

Rating ☆ ☆ ☆ ☆ ☆

Book Title

Author

Nationality

Genre

Year

Pages

Memorable Quote	Page Number

Characters

Plot Summary

Notes

Rating ☆ ☆ ☆ ☆ ☆

Book Title

Author ___________ Nationality ___________

Genre ___________ Year ___________ Pages ___________

Memorable Quote	Page Number

Characters

Plot Summary

Notes

Rating ☆ ☆ ☆ ☆ ☆

Book Title

Author   Nationality

Genre   Year   Pages

Memorable Quote	Page Number

Characters

Plot Summary

Notes

Rating ☆ ☆ ☆ ☆ ☆

Book Title

Author

Nationality

Genre

Year

Pages

Memorable Quote	Page Number

Characters

Plot Summary

Notes

Rating ☆ ☆ ☆ ☆ ☆

Book Title

Author

Nationality

Genre

Year

Pages

Memorable Quote	Page Number

Characters

Plot Summary

Notes

Rating ☆ ☆ ☆ ☆ ☆

Book Title

Author

Nationality

Genre

Year

Pages

Memorable Quote	Page Number

Characters

Plot Summary

Notes

Rating ☆ ☆ ☆ ☆ ☆

Book Title

Author

Nationality

Genre

Year

Pages

Memorable Quote	Page Number

Characters

Plot Summary

Notes

Rating ☆ ☆ ☆ ☆ ☆

Book Title

Author

Nationality

Genre

Year

Pages

Memorable Quote	Page Number

Characters

Plot Summary

Notes

Rating ☆ ☆ ☆ ☆ ☆

Book Title

Author

Nationality

Genre

Year

Pages

Memorable Quote	Page Number

Characters

Plot Summary

Notes

Rating ☆ ☆ ☆ ☆ ☆

Book Title

Author   Nationality

Genre   Year   Pages

Memorable Quote	Page Number

Characters

Plot Summary

Notes

Rating ☆ ☆ ☆ ☆ ☆

Book Title

Author

Nationality

Genre

Year

Pages

Memorable Quote	Page Number

Characters

Plot Summary

Notes

Rating ☆ ☆ ☆ ☆ ☆

Book Title

Author

Nationality

Genre

Year

Pages

Memorable Quote	Page Number

Characters

Plot Summary

Notes

Rating ☆ ☆ ☆ ☆ ☆

Book Title

Author

Nationality

Genre

Year

Pages

Memorable Quote	Page Number

Characters

Plot Summary

Notes

Rating ☆ ☆ ☆ ☆ ☆

Book Title

Author

Nationality

Genre

Year

Pages

Memorable Quote	Page Number

Characters

Plot Summary

Notes

Rating ☆ ☆ ☆ ☆ ☆

Book Title

Author

Nationality

Genre

Year

Pages

Memorable Quote	Page Number

Characters

Plot Summary

Notes

Rating ☆ ☆ ☆ ☆ ☆

Book Title

Author

Nationality

Genre

Year

Pages

Memorable Quote	Page Number

Characters

Plot Summary

Notes

Rating ☆ ☆ ☆ ☆ ☆

Book Title

Author

Nationality

Genre

Year

Pages

Memorable Quote	Page Number

Characters

Plot Summary

Notes

Rating ☆ ☆ ☆ ☆ ☆

Book Title

Author

Nationality

Genre

Year

Pages

Memorable Quote	Page Number

Characters

Plot Summary

Notes

Rating ☆ ☆ ☆ ☆ ☆

Book Title

Author

Nationality

Genre

Year

Pages

Memorable Quote	Page Number

Characters

Plot Summary

Notes

Rating ☆ ☆ ☆ ☆ ☆

Book Title

Author

Nationality

Genre

Year

Pages

Memorable Quote	Page Number

Characters

Plot Summary

Notes

Rating ☆ ☆ ☆ ☆ ☆

Book Title

Author   Nationality

Genre   Year   Pages

Memorable Quote	Page Number

Characters

Plot Summary

Notes

Rating ☆ ☆ ☆ ☆ ☆

Book Title

Author

Nationality

Genre

Year

Pages

Memorable Quote	Page Number

Characters

Plot Summary

Notes

Rating ☆ ☆ ☆ ☆ ☆

Book Title

Author   Nationality

Genre   Year   Pages

Memorable Quote	Page Number

Characters

Plot Summary

Notes

Rating ☆ ☆ ☆ ☆ ☆

Book Title

Author

Nationality

Genre

Year

Pages

Memorable Quote	Page Number

Characters

Plot Summary

Notes

Rating ☆ ☆ ☆ ☆ ☆

Book Title

Author

Nationality

Genre

Year

Pages

Memorable Quote	Page Number

Characters

Plot Summary

Notes

Rating ☆ ☆ ☆ ☆ ☆

Book Title

Author   Nationality

Genre   Year   Pages

Memorable Quote	Page Number

Characters

Plot Summary

Notes

Rating ☆ ☆ ☆ ☆ ☆

Book Title

Author   Nationality

Genre   Year   Pages

Memorable Quote	Page Number

Characters

Plot Summary

Notes

Rating ☆ ☆ ☆ ☆ ☆

Book Title

Author

Nationality

Genre

Year

Pages

Memorable Quote	Page Number

Characters

Plot Summary

Notes

Rating ☆ ☆ ☆ ☆ ☆

Book Title

Author ______________________ Nationality ______________

Genre ______________________ Year ______________ Pages ______

Memorable Quote	Page Number

Characters

Plot Summary

Notes

Rating ☆ ☆ ☆ ☆ ☆

Book Title

Author

Nationality

Genre

Year

Pages

Memorable Quote	Page Number

Characters

Plot Summary

Notes

Rating ☆ ☆ ☆ ☆ ☆

Book Title

Author

Nationality

Genre

Year

Pages

Memorable Quote	Page Number

Characters

Plot Summary

Notes

Rating ☆ ☆ ☆ ☆ ☆

Book Title

Author

Nationality

Genre

Year

Pages

Memorable Quote	Page Number

Characters

Plot Summary

Notes

Rating ☆ ☆ ☆ ☆ ☆

Book Title

Author   Nationality

Genre   Year   Pages

Memorable Quote	Page Number

Characters

Plot Summary

Notes

Rating ☆ ☆ ☆ ☆ ☆

Book Title

Author

Nationality

Genre

Year

Pages

Memorable Quote	Page Number

Characters

Plot Summary

Notes

Rating ☆ ☆ ☆ ☆ ☆

Book Title

Author

Nationality

Genre

Year

Pages

Memorable Quote	Page Number

Characters

Plot Summary

Notes

Rating ☆ ☆ ☆ ☆ ☆